READ ALOUD TALES OF
GANESHA

Ganesha goes to Lunch
and other stories...

Retold by

VANEETA VAID

Nita Mehta
Publications
Enriching Young Minds

LARGE PRINT

READ ALOUD TALES OF
GANESHA

Ganesha goes to Lunch
and other stories...

Nita Mehta
Publications
Enriching Young Minds

LARGE PRINT

READ ALOUD TALES OF
GANESHA

Ganesha goes to Lunch
and other stories...

Distributed by :
NITA MEHTA BOOKS
3A/3, Asaf Ali Road, New Delhi - 02

Distribution Centre :
D16/1, Okhla Industrial Area, Phase-I,
New Delhi - 110020
Tel.: 26813199, 26813200
E-mail: nitamehta.mehta@gmail.com

Contributing Writers:
Subhash Mehta
Tanya Mehta

Editorial & Proofreading:
Rajesh
Ramesh

Nita Mehta Publications

Nita Mehta Publications

Corporate Office
3A/3, Asaf Ali Road, New Delhi 110 002
Phone: +91 11 2325 2948, 2325 0091
Telefax: +91 11 2325 0091
E-mail: nitamehta@nitamehta.com
Website: www.nitamehta.com

Reprint 2014

Printed in India at Infinity Advertising Services (P) Ltd, New Delhi

Editorial and Marketing office
E-159, Greater Kailash II, New Delhi 110 048

Typesetting by National Information Technology Academy
3A/3, Asaf Ali Road, New Delhi 110 002

Price: Rs. 145/-

CONTENTS

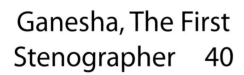

Introduction

Ganesha has a special place in the hearts of people. He is the elephant headed Hindu God. Ganesha is the son of Lord Shiva and Goddess Parvati. He has 108 names. We begin our prayer by taking his name first. Ganesha is associated with many interesting stories. These stories carry strong messages that speak of intelligence, goodwill and honesty. We bring to our young readers, tales that have entertained us for many, many years. These value based stories are accompanied by colourfull illustrations.

GANESHA AND THE CAT

Little Ganesha went: hoppity hop- hop- hop- hop!
Down the mountain path.

Vroommmm! His vehicle arrived!

What vehcle did Ganesha ride?

He rode a mouse!

Quickly sitting 'mouseback,' Ganesha sang,
"Lets goooooo!"

The Mouse raced down the mountains,
with Ganesha on his back!

"Stop.......!"
Ganesha pulled at mouse.

The mouse immediately halted.

Ganesha dismounted and asked,

"H m m m?
Mouse? What
should I play?"

Mouse could think of nothing to suggest, so he was silent.

Ganesha frowned at him.

Mouse looked so sorry for himself! He moved his head here and there!

"Mouse, I am off on my own. You stay here!" trumped Ganesha. Ganesha trotted ahead, leaving Mouse behind.

"Meow-meow-scarrrrrlrllll!"

"Huh?" Ganesha stopped. What was that sound?

"Gasp!" Ganesha spotted a cat in a cave!

mew mew mew...

"Meowwwwwwww!" The cat mewed.

"Giggle- giggle," laughed Ganesha, "You look like a mini tiger?"

The cat mewed, "Meow meow!"

Ganesha reached out to roughly pick up the cat!

"Growwwwwwwlsslssll," the cat protested!

Oh dear, Ganesha was so amused he did not realise he was hurting the cat!

Catching the tail of the cat, Ganesha swung around chortling, "Yayyyyyyyyyyy!" "Scrawwwwlwlwling!" The cat yelped. Ganesha rolled the cat on the ground like a foot ball ,"bump bump bump!"

"Scrawwwwlwlwling!"

"bump bump!"

Soon, Ganesha was tired.

"Toooooooweeeetieeeeee!" He whistled for Mouse.

Screeeeeech! Mouse braked in front of him.

Ganesha quickly sat atop Mouse and returned home.

Ganesha dashed into his home, the cave, at Kailash Mountain.

"Oooooo-ouch-ooooo!"

Ganesha heard his mother moan inside.

"Ma…you are hurt? How did this happen?"

"Yes my son, I am hurt. You did this to me!"

"Me?" Ganesha was puzzled.

"Yes, you! That cat you teased so cruelly? That cat was me!"

"That cat was you? How?" Ganesha was puzzled.

"I had disguised myself as a cat."

"But why?" cried Ganesha impatiently.

"So you and I could play!" explained Parvati.

"Oh!" Ganesha looked ashamed.

"You had no feelings for a poor helpless cat!" Parvati sobbed.

Yes, Ganesha's mother was a goddess. She could change her form to anything she wanted!

Ganesha felt so sad. He thought, 'I hurt an animal without realizing that it had feelings too. My mother made me realize that!'

Ganesha promised never to be cruel to any animal ever again!

GANESHA GOES TO LUNCH

Lord Kuber, the God of wealth, visited Mount Kailash. He wanted to invite Lord Shiva and Goddess Parvati to his house for lunch.

"Ganesha will come for lunch to your house, instead of us!" Lord Shiva announced.

Soon Kuber and Ganesha reached Kuber's luxurious palace. The pillars were made of pure gold and the doors of pure silver.

Everything glittered and glowed. The lunch was a lavish spread.

"Eat up Ganesha…I have plenty…I am rich!" Lord Kuber boasted.

As Ganesha *ate and ate and ate*…Kuber boasted and boasted *and boasted!*

Ganesha kept eating. Lord Kuber kept boasting!

"*Pssssst-pssst, my Lord!?!*" Someone hissed to Lord Kuber.

"Whaaaat?" Kuber asked, startled.

"My Lord, the food has finished!" said the cook from Kuber's kitchen.

"Finished!?!"

"Yes!" nodded the cook, rapidly moving his head up and down.

"Chomp chomp chomp, I am still hungry!" slurped Ganesha, looking up expectantly.

"Go and bring food from my lands…hurry!" Lord Kuber instructed his helpers.

"Food…more food…hungry…foood!" Ganesha cried.

All the food from Lord Kuber's lands was presented to Ganehsa.

Ganesha ate every morsel, then looked up for more.

"Ganesha, the food is over!" Lord Kuber quaked.

"What?! I am hungry!" Ganesha jumped up and began to eat every article in sight. He ate up Lord Kuber's jewels, coins and silver ware!

He chomped through the palace doors, pillars, furniture! Soon, there was nothing left to eat!

"*I will eat you!*" Ganesha screamed, pouncing on Kuber.

"Helppppppp! Aaaaaaargh! No Ganesha!"

Kuber screamed and fled.

"I am hungry! I will eat you!" Ganesha shouted back.

Kuber was so frightened. He ran as fast as his legs could carry him. Kuber ran towards the oceans, but Ganesha reached there.

Kuber escaped towards the plains. *Ganesha was there too!*

Finally, Kuber reached the cave where Lord Shiva and Parvati were. He fell at Lord Shiva's feet, "Pant, pant hufff-pufff-s-save m-e! Ganesha wants to eat me…!"

"Calm down. The boy is hungry. Here, give him this rice."

Saying this, Lord Shiva poured a handful of roasted rice into Kuber's palm.

""What?" a puzzled Kuber stared at the rice. "*He is really hungry, this will not be enough*!" Kuber wailed.

Suddenly, Ganesha charged at Kuber.

In panic, Kuber gave Ganesha the rice.

"Gulp!" Ganesha swallowed the rice. "Hmmm, now I am not hungry! Thank you!" Ganesha said to Kuber.

Kuber was embarrassed. He understood the lesson that Lord Shiva wanted to teach him. What was the lesson? Boasting always leads to trouble.

HOW THE MOON LOST ITS SHINE?

Can you imagine if the light of the moon was switched off? I am sure you cannot imagine that! That day, it was Lord Ganesha's birthday! He was so happy! And do you know what? Ganesha ate five full trays of delicious 'laddoos'.

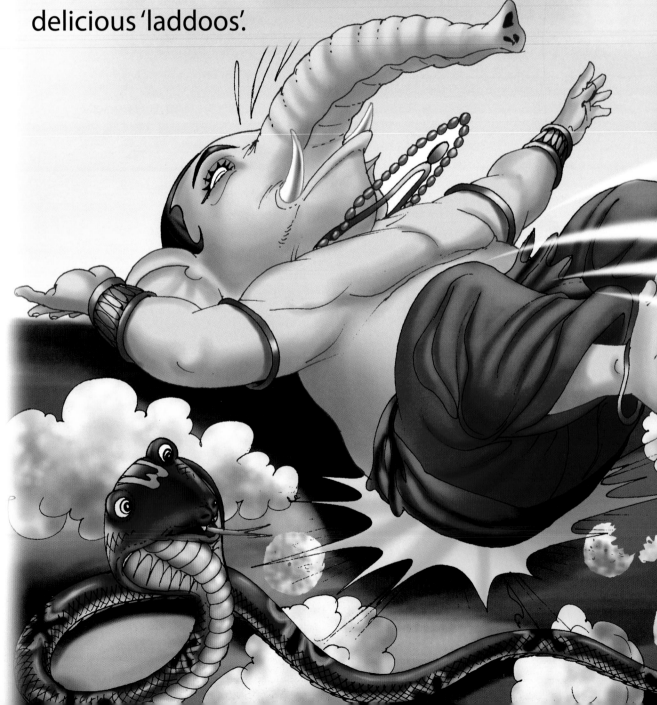

His stomach was so full that he could not move! "If I move, my stomach will burst!" Ganesha informed Mouse.

"Come Mouse, take me home!" Ganesha carefully sat on his mouse and they were off: Vroooooooooooom!

Alas! There was an accident.

What happened?

A snake was crossing the road.

Mouse failed to see the snake and

Dhuuuuuumb…

he tripped and tumbled!

Ganesha went flying. Oh dear, all the laddoos flew out:

Bing bing bing bing bing…

ha ha ha hee hee

Five full trays of laddoos came soaring out from Ganesha's belly!

Ganesha quickly stood up and hurriedly put back all the laddoos in his tummy. He was very embarrassed, you see.

ha ha ha hee hee

He then scooped up the snake and tied his stomach so the laddoos would not spill out again!

Oh yes! *Ganesha used the snake as a belt!*

"Giggle giggle-ha-ha-ha-ha-hee-tee heeee-heeee, using a snake as a belt, ha-ha-ha-ha!"

Who was laughing at Ganesha?

Oh oh, it was the Moon laughing at Ganesha!

Ganesha did not like that at all!

"Ha-ha-ha-ha-hee-teeee!" the Moon giggled uncontrollably!

"*Moon quiet!*" boomed Ganesha, angry at being laughed at.

But the Moon would not stop giggling at all!

"*Moon, it is very rude to tease…*" *saying* that, Ganesha broke a part of his left tusk and threw it at the moon!

Zingggggggggg!

The tusk hit the Moon square in the face and his light switched off!

"You remain without lights now!" Ganesha shouted angrily.

Ssssssssshhhhhh!

Darkness fell all over the world!

People were very unhappy. Well, you would be too if there was no moon light on a dark night-right?

All the Gods begged Ganesha to bring back the moon light.

Ganesha's anger had calmed down by now, so he shrugged and said, "Alright! I will give the Moon his light back."

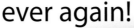

Wangggg! The moon got his light back.

The moon sheepishly thanked Ganesha and promised never to tease anyone ever again!

"Thank you!"

THE RACE

"Children, gather here. We have something for you!"
Parvati called her sons, Kartekeya and Ganesha.

The boys ran towards her, "Thud thud thud!"

Lord Shiva was sitting beside her too.

"Children, we have a rare fruit here. See."

A fruit radiantly glowed in her palm! The boys had never seen a fruit like that!

Ganesha cried, "I should get the fruit first! Give it to me!" Ganesha stretched his hand. Sigh! So did Kartekeya! Oh dear! An argument started between the two.

"Stop!" Lord Shiva bellowed.

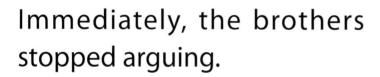

Immediately, the brothers stopped arguing.

"Between the two of you, whosoever can encircle the universe the fastest, will get the fruit," announced Shiva.

In no time, Kartekeya hopped on to his peacock and flew away!

Ganesha too sat on his mouse, but he did not run. Instead, he began to encircle both his parents. Round and round, Ganesha swirled. Finally, he stopped.

His parents stared at him amazed. "Father-Mother, award me the fruit. I have encircled the universe," said Ganesha.

Meanwhile, Kartekeya had returned too.

Curiously, they all asked Ganesha what he meant.

"You represent the entire existence, Mother and Father. So encircling you means I have toured the universe!"

"Ganesha that is so intelligent of you!" Lord Shiva clapped.

Thus, the rare fruit was given to Ganesha.

Ganesha blushing

HOW GANESHA HELPED THE CAUVERY RIVER TO FLOW

Lord Shiva ordered Rishi Agastya to take water from his matted hair and create a river called Cauvery on earth. The location was in the south; this part of the earth was very thirsty, you see!

Agastya, however, trapped Cauvery in the small urn he was carrying. Now, why would he do that? Well, it seems river Cauvery *did not show respect to Rishi Agastya*. That really annoyed him. So, even though he came to earth, he did not release Cauvery from the urn.

That was not nice. Humans were suffering without her refreshing waters. The Gods decided to ask Ganesha for help. Ganesha readily agreed.

He disguised himself as a little boy and made friends with Rishi Agastya.

Not suspecting anything, Agastya allowed Ganesha (the little boy), to walk with him. Ganesha noticed the urn in the Rishi's hand, but said nothing. Soon, Agastya wanted to go somewhere. He addressed the little boy, "Here keep this urn safe for me. I will return in a while."

Ganesha quickly grasped the urn. He wisely selected a spot to place the urn.

He then transformed himself into a crow and perched himself on the edge of the urn's mouth.

"Shooooo-shoooooo!" yelled Agastya on his return. He was horrified to see the urn on the ground. He could not see the boy either. Angrily, he shooed the crow.

Twunggggg!

The crow (who was actually Ganesha) flew off and in the process, he tripped the urn!

WHOOOOOOOOOOOOOOOOOOOOOOOOOOOSH!

Cauvery flew out in huge, wavy gushes. She filled her waters in and beyond the spot, quenching the thirst of the parched earth. This spot is called Talacauvery.

GANESHA, THE FIRST STENOGRAPHER

"I need to write a very long and beautiful poem called the Mahabharata," said Ved Vyasa to Ganesha.

"But I cannot write and think at the same time. Ganesha, may I request you to assist me to write the poem? All you need to do is to write out whatever I recite. Of course, you must understand whatever you write too!"

"I would like to help. But there is one condition. When reciting the poem, please do not waste time. Please don't take any breaks," answered Ganesha.

Ved Vyasa readily agreed and began to recite his poem. Ganesha diligently took dictation, while Ved Vyasa chanted the poem.

Oh dear, Ganesha wrote so fast that Ved Vyasa was finding it difficult to keep up.

Yes, Ganesha wrote so fast that Ved Vyasa could not even take a break to breathe. He was struggling to breathe. Ved Vyasa decided to do something about this since he was going blue in the face.

'I will die, if I do not take a break and catch my breath,' thought a panicky Ved Vyasa. 'I must think of something.'

Ved Vyasa then created a very complicated and tricky stanza for the verses. For a split second, Ganesha was confused and he paused to understand before writing.

Whoosh!

In those fractions of time, Ved Vyasa inhaled gulps of air. And so whenever Vyasa needed a break, he would narrate a difficult stanza. Ganesha would stall to understand the verse and Vyasa swiftly gasped in a breath!

Thus, the original *Mahabharata* contains many difficult stanzas placed at intervals throughout the length of the epic.

By writing the verses of the great poem *Mahabharata*, Lord Ganesha became the first stenographer in the world! He had taken down the largest book ever composed, dictated by sage Vyasa.

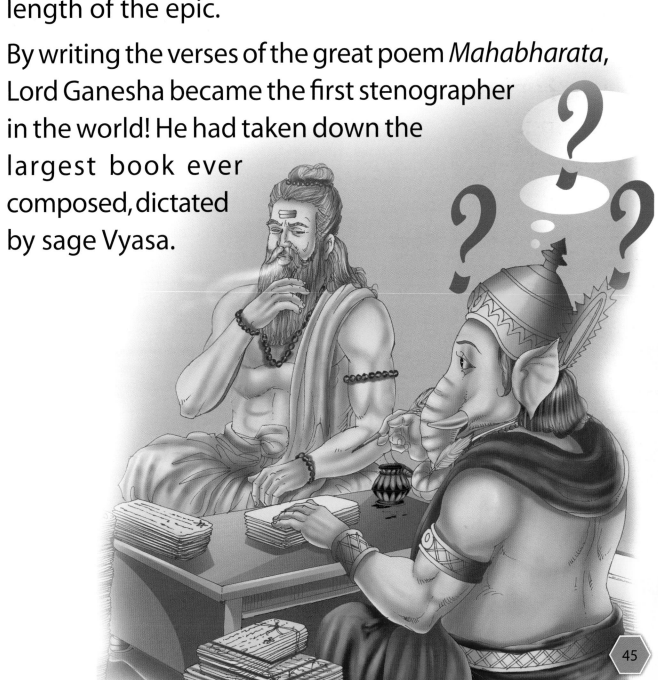

Activity

COUNT THE BOOKS AND WRITE THE TOTAL.

1. + = __6__

2. + = __4__

3. + = __7__

4. + = __5__

5. + = __3__

DID YOU KNOW?

Ganesha has 108 names. Some of his lesser known names and meanings are listed below.

NAMES OF GANESHA

S. No.	Name	Meaning
1.	Avaneesh	Lord of the whole World
2.	Bhalchandra	Moon-Crested Lord
3.	Chaturbhuj	One who has Four Arms
4.	Devendrashika	Protector of All Gods
5.	Ekadanta	Single-Tusked Lord
6.	Gajanana	Elephant-Faced Lord
7.	Haridra	One who is Golden Colored
8.	Kriti	Lord of Music
9.	Lambodara	The Huge Bellied Lord
10.	Muktidaya	Bestower of Eternal Bliss

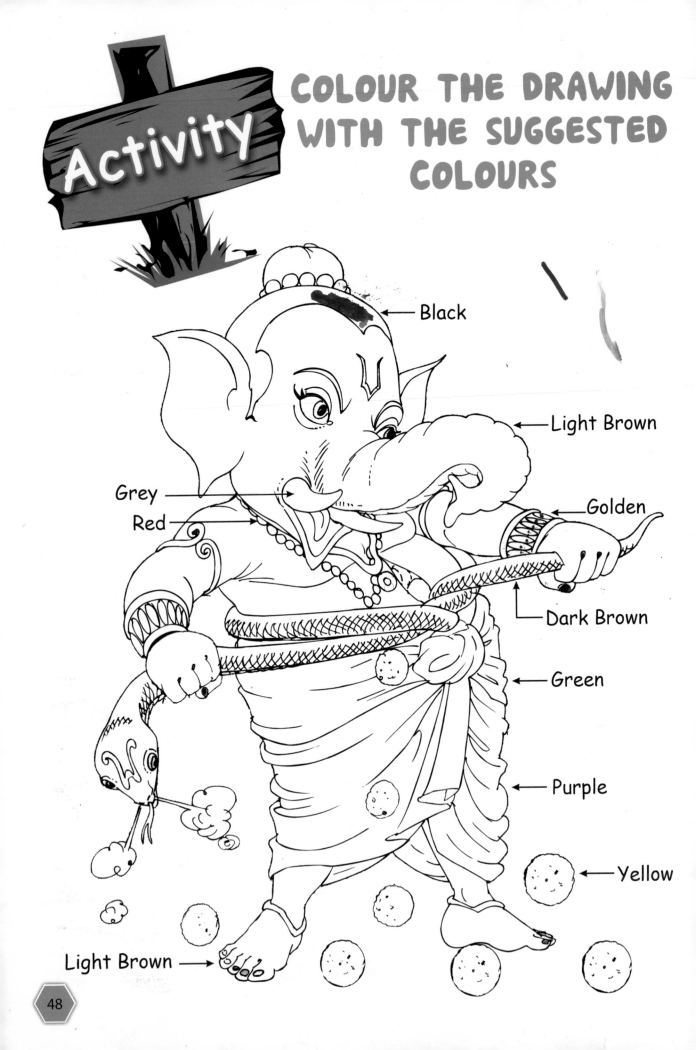

Activity

COLOUR THE DRAWING WITH THE SUGGESTED COLOURS

Black

Light Brown

Grey

Red

Golden

Dark Brown

Green

Purple

Yellow

Light Brown